www.enchantedlion.com

First English-language edition, published in 2019 by Enchanted Lion Books,
67 West Street, 317A, Brooklyn, NY 11222
Text and Illustrations copyright © 2005 by Kaya Doi.
English language translation © 2019 Enchanted Lion Books
English translation rights arranged with Alicekan Ltd. through Japan UNI Agency, Inc.
All rights reserved under International and Pan-American Copyright Conventions.
A CIP record is on file with the Library of Congress. ISBN 978-1-59270-278-7
Printed in China in May 2019 by RR Donnelley Asia Printing Solutions Ltd.
3 5 7 9 10 8 6 4 2

It's morning and the birds are singing.
Chirri and Chirra decide to go for a bicycle ride.

Kaya Doi

Chirri & Chirra

On the Town

Translated from Japanese by

David Boyd

ENCHANTED LION BOOKS

NEW YORK

Dring-dring, dring-dring!
They pedal through town
until they arrive at a small shop.

It's a shop with spools of thread
and yarn in every color!

They're all so pretty…

"What do you think of these?
They just came in."

Cotton yarn dyed with flowers?
Just look at the colors!
Chirri and Chirra choose their favorites.

Chirri picks camellia and poppy.

Chirra picks marigold and violet.

Dring-dring, dring-dring!
They ride through the woods.

Dring-dring, dring-dring!
The old town has so many shops.

The weaver is just about to open for the day.

Inside, she has many different
kinds of cloth.

"What pretty yarn! I'll make something for you.
It won't take very long."

They listen to the weaver work.
Whish, clack, whish, clack.

"Wake up, Chirri and Chirra. They're ready."

"I hope you like the fringe
and grape beads."

What lovely scarves!
When Chirri and Chirra wrap
them around their necks, they
can faintly smell the flowers.

They're about to ride home with their new scarves,
when they hear *Chiri-chirira... Chiri-chirira...*
Is somebody calling their names?

It's coming from over there.

Dring-dring, dring-dring!
They wind along the narrow path.

At the end, they find a
beautiful house.

"Why, hello! We've just made the most delicious soup. Please, come in."

Chirri and Chirra
are invited into a
warm room.

They are offered a two-tone pumpkin and potato soup, chock-full of nuts and mushrooms.

Chirri and Chirra have seconds, thirds, and even fourths.

Once they've eaten their fill, they hear it again.
Chiri-chirira... Chiri-chirira...

It sounds like it's out back.

They pull the curtain and find
a magnificent rose garden.

Chiri-chirira... Chiri-chirira...

It's coming from beyond the arbor.

A bird's nest!

"Welcome, welcome!
Our party is just about to begin!
We have so much to celebrate."

Wow!

Looking closer, they see three baby birds,
nuzzled up against their parents' bellies.

Chiri-chirira, chiri-chirira!

Look! Up in the sky. All the birds
have come for the celebration.

Chiri-chirira, chiri-chirira!
A beautiful dusk settles over the town.

Born in Tokyo, Kaya Doi graduated with a degree in design from Tokyo Zokei University. She got her start in picture books by attending the Atosaki Juku Workshop, a program at a Tokyo bookshop. Prolific and popular, Doi has created many wonderful books. She now lives in Chiba Prefecture and maintains a strong interest in environmental and animal welfare issues.

David Boyd is Assistant Professor of Japanese at the University of North Carolina at Charlotte. His translations have appeared in *Monkey Business International*, *Granta*, and *Words Without Borders*.